Skeleton Crew

ALLAN AHLBERG • ANDRÉ AMSTUTZ

PUFFIN

On a dark dark night,
on a dark dark sea,
in a dark dark boat
three skeletons float . . .

on a holiday.

The big one is dozing
in his deckchair.
"Zzz!"

Zzz!

The dog one is dozing
in his hammock.
"Zzz!"
The little one is fishing.

I've got a bite!

. . . and it throws *him* back.

Splash!

The next night
in the dark boat
under the starry sky
the big one has a try.

The big skeleton catches a little fish
and throws it back.
He catches a big fish and keeps it.
He catches a bigger fish . . .

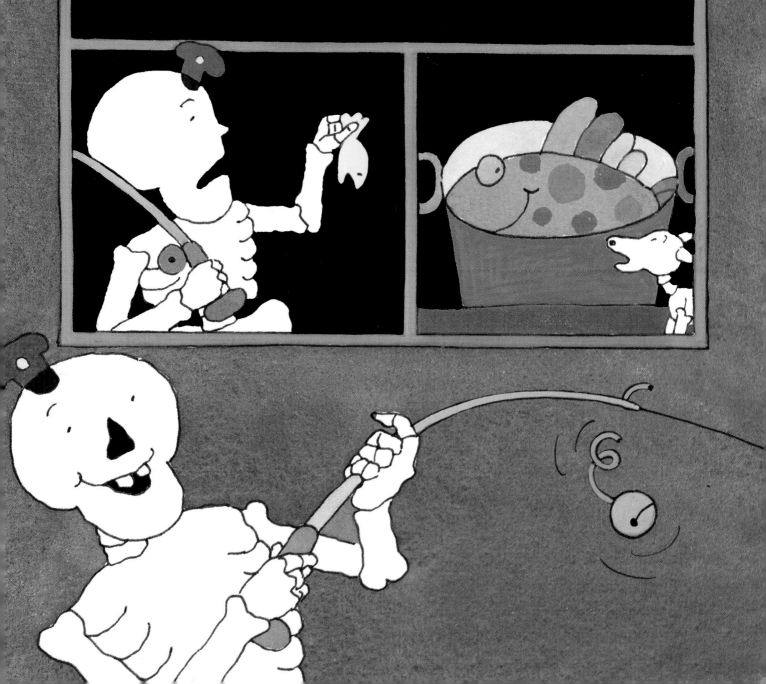

And – "Yo – ho – ho!" –
the *pirates* come.

The pirates climb aboard
looking for treasure.
They steal the deckchair
and the hammock.

Bye-bye!

They steal the fishing rod
and the catfish.
"Miaow!"
They steal . . . the boat!

That's a nice rod – I'll have that!

nothing happens.

But the *next* night,
under a starry sky
and over the deep blue sea,
the skeletons spy . . . a tree.
"Yippee!"

On the island
the big skeleton
finds a parrot.
"Pretty Polly!"

The little one finds a coconut.
"Clonk!"
And the dog finds a crab.

Also, *somebody* finds them.

The next night a lot happens.
A storm blows up.
The thunder crashes,
the lightning flashes,
the wind howls
and the dog howls too.
"Howl!"

As quick as a blink
the raft is blown
across the foam . . .

The End (or is it?)

The End

PUFFIN BOOKS

Published by the Penguin Group
Penguin Books Ltd, 80 Strand, London WC2R 0RL, England
Penguin Group (USA) Inc., 375 Hudson Street, New York, New York 10014, USA
Penguin Group (Canada), 10 Alcorn Avenue, Toronto, Ontario, Canada M4V 3B2
(a division of Pearson Penguin Canada Inc.)
Penguin Ireland, 25 St Stephen's Green, Dublin 2, Ireland (a division of Penguin Books Ltd)
Penguin Group (Australia), 250 Camberwell Road, Camberwell, Victoria 3124, Australia
(a division of Pearson Australia Group Pty Ltd)
Penguin Books India Pvt Ltd, 11 Community Centre, Panchsheel Park, New Delhi – 110 017, India
Penguin Group (NZ), cnr Airborne and Rosedale Roads, Albany, Auckland 1310, New Zealand
(a division of Pearson New Zealand Ltd)
Penguin Books (South Africa) (Pty) Ltd, 24 Sturdee Avenue, Rosebank, Johannesburg 2196, South Africa

Penguin Books Ltd, Registered Offices: 80 Strand, London WC2R 0RL, England

www.penguin.com

First published by William Heinemann Ltd 1992
First published in Puffin Books 2005
3 5 7 9 10 8 6 4 2

Text copyright © Allan Ahlberg, 1992
Illustrations copyright © André Amstutz, 1992
All rights reserved

The moral right of the author and illustrator has been asserted

Set in Bembo
Manufactured in China

British Library Cataloguing in Publication Data
A CIP catalogue record for this book is available from the British Library

ISBN-13: 978-0-140-56683-3
ISBN-10: 0-140-56683-X